With thanks to my family: Benedict, George and Nigel.
Also to Jane Green, Sarah Davies from the Holy Trinity Pewley
Down School in Guildford and the National Autistic Society.
And for all the encouragement and support from Denise Johnstone-Burt
and all at Walker Books, and my agent Laura Cecil.

First published 2016 by Walker Books Ltd
87 Vauxhall Walk, London SE11 5HJ

2 4 6 8 10 9 7 5 3 1

© 2016 Melanie Walsh

The right of Melanie Walsh to be identified as author/illustrator of this work has been
asserted by her in accordance with the Copyright, Designs and Patents Act 1988

This book has been typeset in WB Walsh

Printed in China

British Library Cataloguing in Publication Data:
a catalogue record for this book is available from the British Library

ISBN 978-1-4063-4445-5

www.walker.co.uk

ISAAC AND HIS AMAZING ASPERGER SUPERPOWERS!

melanie walsh

WALKER BOOKS
AND SUBSIDIARIES
LONDON • BOSTON • SYDNEY • AUCKLAND

My name is Isaac and I'm a superhero!

You might think I look just like everyone else, but I've got special superpowers that make me slightly different to my brother and the other kids at school. However some children don't understand this and call me names.

My superhero brain is fantastic and remembers loads of things. I love to tell people interesting facts I know,

cat
rocket
snake

but sometimes they just walk away!

My superpowers give me lots of energy and I love to bounce around on my trampoline for hours! It makes me feel happy.

Sometimes at school my teacher asks if I want to play football. But I don't like running around and superheroes don't like sticky mud.

Oh ...
hello.

Because I'm a superhero
I have lots of things
to think about.
I try to remember
to say hello to
people I know, but
sometimes I forget.
I'm not being rude.

My pets understand me and my
superpowers and I love them.
I find it easy to talk to them
and they always listen.

Because my teacher knows I'm a superhero she lets me fidget with my special toy in class. It helps me feel calm and I can listen better.

"Meow," said the little cat.
"Shh," said Mummy.

Shh!

As a superhero I like to tell people what they look like, as they might not know!

My mum says that I should try and keep these thoughts in my head as I might upset people.

Superheroes listen carefully, but sometimes get confused. When my brother told me that my tummy would go POP if I ate too much ...

I believed him!
I don't really get
jokes like this.

My ears can hear super well.
I can even hear the buzzing
that some lights make in
shops. This makes my ears
really hurt and I feel upset.

I feel scared
when I look people
in the eyes.

My dad taught me a good
superhero trick. I just look
at people's foreheads instead.
It really works!

5 6 7 8

Superheroes are really good at spotting things.
At playtime if there isn't a game I want to play
I like to use my super-vision to find interesting
things that other people haven't seen!

You may not have guessed, but I'm not really a superhero. I have Asperger's (it rhymes with hamburgers) which is a kind of autism.

You can't catch it. It just means my brain works a little differently.

But I do love playing superheroes with my brother. He understands me and now you do too!